...ILY NEWS

...OO SHOCKED!

...HOLE DISCOVERED IN FENCE!

...ANIMALS MISSING

This morning, the zookeepers were shocked to discover a large hole in the fence.

"I COULD BARELY BELIEVE MY EYES!" exclaimed head zookeeper Theodore Wilde.

Some animals are missing and the zookeepers have begun a search.

"...WE'RE BEARING UP UNDER ...RAIN," said the team. Any ...public who may ...

The search will be ha... "WE WILL GRIN... BEAR IT," com... The zoo will... closed for... but hope...

Happy car... said h... carek... we...

For Vanny, Mark, and Andrea,
and all their loved ones—A.S.

ISBN 978-0-545-51746-1

Text and illustrations copyright © 2011 by Adam Stower.
All rights reserved. Published by Orchard Books, an imprint of Scholastic Inc.,
by arrangement with Templar Publishing, Surrey, United Kingdom. ORCHARD BOOKS and design are
registered trademarks of Watts Publishing Group, Ltd., used under license. SCHOLASTIC and
associated logos are trademarks and/or registered trademarks of Scholastic Inc.

12 11 10 9 8 7 6 5 4 3 2 1   13 14 15 16 17 18/0

Printed in the U.S.A.   40

This edition first printing, September 2013

Silly Doggy!

Silly Doggy!

by Adam Stower

SCHOLASTIC INC.

One morning, Lily saw something wonderful in her garden.

It was big, brown, and hairy.

It had four legs, a tail, and a big, wet nose,

and Lily had ALWAYS wanted one. . . .

Up close, he was quite big . . .

for a dog.

And a bit grumpy, too.

But Lily thought
he was lovely.

He just needed someone to look after him,
someone like Lily. So that's just what she did.

After their busy day together,

Lily and Doggy made it back home.

Doggy was so much fun, Lily was sure that Mom

would let her keep him.

She didn't.

Mom said that Doggy must have a home of his own, with someone who must be missing him.

Lily supposed she was right. Probably.

So, to help Doggy's owners find him,
Lily made a poster. . . .

FOUND!

One **very** silly doggy.

Color: brown

Size: big and shaggy

Tail: short

Paws: ~~big~~ **very** big

Legs: yes

Tummy: rumbly

He likes going to the park . . .

but he doesn't like to walk.

He's no good at tricks . . .

and he's terrible at playing fetch.

does what you tell him.

He can get sticky and mucky,
and he doesn't like bath time.

But when he's washed, he looks very pretty.

His favorite thing is scratching.

My favorite thing is him.

— Lily
xo

When the poster was ready,

Lily and Doggy went out

to put it up.

Secretly, Lily hoped no one would see it.

But, of course, someone did.

That night, even though she knew
he was happy back in his own home,
Lily felt sad that Doggy was gone.

But, the next morning,

she saw something

WONDERFUL

in the garden. . . .

...the zoo were delighted by ...some good news: ...eturn of one of their favorite ...and now animals. "He's learned some new tricks," said the head zookeeper, "and will do anything for a tummy rub!"

The public is warned that other ...mals from the zoo are still at large.

PURR-FECT SCORE

Local girl Lily and "Kitty" were the proud winners of this year's cat show. "What Kitty lacked in obedience, she made up for in teeth!" said the judge. Lily said she would use the prize — a season ticket to the zoo — to visit a very special friend.